Madison's
TELL-ALL
JOURNAL

ISBN 978-1-0980-0069-1 (paperback)
ISBN 978-1-0980-0070-7 (digital)

Christian Faith Publishing, Inc.
832 Park Avenue
Meadville, PA 16335
www.christianfaithpublishing.com

Printed in the United States of America

BOOK 1

Madison's
TELL-ALL
JOURNAL

Christy Mollet

Taylor Nelson's beautiful emerald-green eyes widened with devilish delight.

"Perfect," she said, reading a particularly juicy entry inside the purple notebook she found on the classroom floor. "Well it looks like little Miss Madison isn't as innocent as she claims," Taylor scoffed, tossing the tell-all book into her backpack.

Madison Links and her two best friends, Hallie Jonshire and Jaime Benson, lingered outside the front door of Sorenville Elementary School. The fresh spring air was just what they needed after a long day of school. The girls were happy to be done with their day so they could finalize their plans for their exciting weekend at Jaime's house.

"I can't wait until this weekend," Hallie exclaimed, sitting on the newly-painted handrail. "We're going to have so much fun on our trip to the zoo."

"I know, but don't forget about our sleepover too!" nine-year-old Madison squealed as her frizzy blond curls bounced in the wind. "Only one more day!"

"Be excited all you want, but I'm not allowed to have anyone over until my room is cleaned," Jaime said, picking up her books off the concrete steps.

"Then you better start cleaning now," Hallie suggested. "That way everything will be ready by Friday evening."

"I guess," Jaime said. "But you don't know my mom. She hates dust, and if she finds any, I'll be grounded for a month, and the whole weekend will be canceled."

"Oh, Jaime," Hallie said, shaking her head. "You're such a drama queen! Just get it done and then you won't have to worry so much!"

Jaime smiled and stuck out her tongue at Hallie.

"It will be fine, Jaime. I know it will," Madison answered, reassuringly. At least she hoped it would.

The girls picked up their stuff and started down the sidewalk. Madison heard the door slam and turned around to see Taylor Nelson walking toward them. Taylor's shifty smile made Madison uneasy. And as hard as she tried not to be, Madison had been jealous of Taylor since she moved to their small town of Sorenville a year ago. She felt like Taylor was always trying to take her two best friends away from her.

"Hey, Hallie! Hey, Jaime!" Taylor called as her beautiful, perfect red hair glistened in the sunlight. "What are you girls doing this fine afternoon?" she asked them while ignoring Madison.

"Walking home," Madison answered sharply. She tried to keep walking, but Hallie and Jaime stopped. She hoped Jaime and Hallie wouldn't say too much to Taylor about the details of their upcoming weekend.

"You want to walk with us?" Hallie asked. "We don't mind. Do we girls?"

"Not at all," Jaime said, smiling.

Madison's face dropped. *Great*, she thought. *Now Taylor is walking home with us.* Madison disliked herself for feeling this way, but there was something about Taylor that she didn't like.

Madison suddenly realized that Taylor was staring at her. She squirmed as Taylor turned to Hallie and Jaime and asked, "What are you doing this weekend? My parents are going to the country club, and I thought you girls could join me?" She glared toward Madison.

"Oh, we would," Jaime said. "But Madison and Hallie are going with me to the zoo this weekend. Sleepover included." She smiled at her two friends.

Madison was mortified. She wished that she could shove those words back into Jaime's mouth, but instead she kept silent.

"Yep!" Hallie stated. "We are super excited!"

"Well, I can't believe that you would invite Madison after what she wrote about the two of you in her journal," Taylor stated, pulling the book out of her backpack.

Madison's eyes widened as she recognized the bright purple journal her mother gave her last Christmas. She wasn't sure how Taylor got ahold of it, but she wanted it back *now*!

"What are you talking about, Taylor?" Jaime asked, folding her arms.

"Wait! What journal?" Hallie questioned, looking at Taylor intently.

"This one right here," Taylor said, holding it up for the girls to see.

Madison's heart pounded as she saw her personal thoughts in the hands of her enemy.

"Give it back!" Madison screamed as she reached for it. She missed, falling down and ripping her favorite blue jeans.

Looking back at Madison, Taylor opened up to the page that she knew would damage Madison's reputation with her friends.

"That's mine, Taylor," Madison whimpered as her cheeks turned red. Suddenly, Madison felt more self-conscious than she ever had.

"If you must know, I was walking by the messiest desk in fourth grade when I accidentally bumped into it. This book fell out and just happened to open to these horrible, horrible words about you two. I mean I had to pick it up to see who it belonged to," Taylor said, clutching it to her chest. "I knew it had to be your dear friend, Madison's journal," she said sarcastically.

Madison lunged for her journal once again as Taylor stepped aside, then she continued on.

"Especially when I saw what she wrote. In fact, I'll even read it to you girls.

"'July 12: Jaime and Hallie are always trying to act cool. I can't believe they left me out today! I called to see what Jaime was doing, and her mom said that she and Hallie had just left together. So once again they leave me out of their plans! Sometimes I don't want to be friends with them. You know, Journal, sometimes I feel that they care more about themselves than me!'" Taylor said with a satisfactory look.

Madison stared at Taylor, tears stinging her eyes. How could Taylor do something so horrible?

"That's silly," Hallie said. "Madison would never write that…would you?"

"Well…I…I," Madison said, trying to form a sentence that wouldn't come out.

"So *you* did write it," Jaime said, walking up to Madison. "You mean, Taylor's telling the truth?"

"Yeah," Madison answered, looking Jaime in the eyes. "But that was over a year ago. No one was ever supposed to see it! But—" She glared right at Taylor.

"No, Madison! No excuses! Someone did see it!" Hallie yelled, her eyes full of tears. "And now we know how you really feel about us."

"Yeah, if that's the way you feel, Madison Links, then consider yourself uninvited!" Jaime shouted.

"Wait, let me explain," Madison wailed as she followed after them.

"Forget about it, Madison. Just leave us alone," Hallie said, walking away with her arm around Jaime.

As Madison watched her angry friends turn the corner, she began crying harder.

Taylor looked Madison up and down. "I guess you three weren't as close as you thought," she said in an arrogant tone.

"Why would you do this to me?" Madison asked, wiping away her tears, while more flowed. "That was uncalled for, Taylor!"

"Why did you write it in the first place?" Taylor hissed. "I would *never* do something like that to my two best friends."

"I-I-don't know," Madison stammered. "I never meant for anyone to see it."

"Well, I saw it," Taylor said. "And I thought they needed to know the kind of friend you really are."

Just then the door opened, and Principal Meyers appeared.

"Is everything okay here?" Principal Meyers asked, pushing his glasses up. "I thought I heard yelling."

"Nope," Taylor lied. "Everything's fine now!" Taylor waited until he went back inside. Then smirking, she tossed the journal at Madison. It fell to the ground, bending some of the pages in different directions.

"Oops!" Taylor said, giggling. "Guess you dropped your journal again."

Madison picked up the dog-eared book as she watched Taylor skip away in delight. Her emotions were all over the place. She was so angry at Taylor, yet she was sad and heartbroken because she was scared that she had lost her best friends forever. But she was more angry at herself for accidentally grabbing her journal this morning along with her homework.

Madison shoved the purple tell-all book down into her bag and walked down the street. As she got closer to Destin Street, she saw Hallie, Jaime, and Taylor. They were talking among themselves. As Madison walked past them on the other side of the street, she tried smiling at Jaime and Hallie. They just glared at her and whispered to each other. Up until now, Madison had felt secure in her friendship with Hallie and Jaime.

As the afternoon slowly turned into the evening, Madison tried to keep herself busy by watching television with her two brothers but everything they watched reminded her of her horrible day. After a relatively quiet dinner, Madison tried to complete her social studies worksheet but soon gave up. As hard as she tried, she couldn't concentrate on anything.

Madison let her mind flood back to the first time she met Hallie and Jaime during their preschool days. Madison smiled when she remembered accidentally knocking the jar of opened paste onto Jaime's new shoes. Madison wept because she made Jaime mad, and Jaime cried because there was paste all over her patented leather shoes. Hallie grabbed paper towels and cleaned up the mess. Madison smiled as she thought how even back then the girls cared for one another. From that moment on, nothing could separate them.

Madison sighed as she came back to reality. *Now they won't talk to me*, she thought. She looked at the clock on her bedside table. It was seven forty-five, and time for her to get ready for bed. She picked up her homework and tried shoving it in her backpack, but her math book got caught on something. She reached into find her journal, once again causing her problems.

"You stupid book," she said, picking it up. She opened it up to the page Taylor read. Madison reread the entry. She stopped, as she realized there was more.

"But, Journal, no matter what, Hallie and Jaime really do mean the world to me. I don't know what I would do without them." Madison's jaw dropped. Taylor didn't read the rest of it! Again her anger raged toward Taylor! How could she lie to Jaime and Hallie like that?

She frantically ran downstairs to use the phone, knocking her backpack and jacket off the back of her desk chair. She had to tell Jaime and Hallie what she finished writing that day, but when she got to the living room, her mother was using the phone.

Madison sadly walked upstairs as the tears formed again. Closing her bedroom door, she wiped her eyes and got ready for bed. She lay back against her pillow and closed her eyes, but all she could see was Taylor waving the journal in the air.

There was a knock on her door.

"Sweetie?" her mother said, coming into her room. "I was just coming in to tell you good night."

"Oh, okay," Madison said, sitting up in bed. She would rather pull the covers over her head and forget the world than to have a conversation with anyone right now.

"Honey, is everything okay?" her mom asked. "You've been awfully quiet since you came home from school today."

"Yeah, I'm fine," Madison said quietly. "I just have a lot on my mind."

"Do you want to talk about it?" her mother inquired, moving Madison's hair out of her face.

"No, I'll be all right," Madison answered, smoothing out the flowered comforter on her bed.

"Okay, well, you get some sleep. Your father will be in as soon as he gets your brother Ryan to fall asleep."

Madison nodded. As her mother closed the door, she tried to get comfortable again. Across the hall, she could hear eleven-year-old Jason yelling at Ryan to go to sleep. She sighed.

"Madison, are you still awake?" her father asked, opening her door.

The light from the hall burst in, highlighting the wall of pictures of Madison and her friends.

"Yes, Daddy," Madison answered, sitting up again.

"Well, I just wanted to tuck you in," he said, kissing the top of her head.

She hugged him tightly. The smell of his cologne comforted her as she lay back down.

"Well, you get some sleep. Tomorrow is your sleepover at Jaime's," her father said, winking at her.

She just smiled, afraid to tell him what was really going on. He blew Madison a kiss, then turned off the light and closed the door behind him. Madison again erupted into tears. Her heart was heavy with the burden of losing two friends in one day. She fell asleep crying and praying that God would somehow fix this situation.

The next morning Madison could hear her family moving around downstairs. She quickly dressed, combed her unkempt curly hair, stuck a headband in, and headed downstairs for breakfast. The smell of pancakes and bacon filled the house. She flopped into the kitchen chair, leaning her backpack against the wall.

"Good morning, Madison," her mother said. "Would you like some chocolate chip pancakes?"

"Yes, please." Madison said politely. She watched her brothers eat. They shoveled it in like they were at a pie-eating contest.

Seven-year-old Ryan was sticky, with chocolate smeared across his face. "And they're yummy!" he chimed in while shoving another big bite into his mouth.

"Ummm…yay," she answered, disgusted by how her little brother looked.

"Hey, Maddie," her older brother Jason said, interrupting her thoughts. "Will you hand me some more butter?"

"Here," Madison said, getting huffy.

"What's wrong with you?" Jason asked, sitting back in his chair.

"Nothing. Just leave me alone, okay?" Madison said, slamming her fork down and running out of the room.

Madison threw herself onto her unmade bed as her stuffed elephant, Trunk, fell off. She sniffled as she picked him up. She rubbed the tag that was on his ear as she smiled. She couldn't help thinking about the day she received it from Jaime.

"Congratulations on accepting Jesus as your Savior. Remember God is always with you!"

She punched the elephant, then threw him across the room. Her eyes flooded with tears again as she replayed yesterday's event in her head. Frustrated with everything, she laid her head down into her pillows and sobbed.

"What am I going to do?" Madison asked herself. She knew she had to get her mind off her problem and quick since it was almost time to leave for school. She sat up and wiped her eyes, but in her mind she kept seeing the hurt in Jaime and Hallie's faces.

Finally, she couldn't take it anymore. She looked up at the ceiling and begged God to help her.

"God, please forgive me for writing those awful things in my journal. I'm so sorry for what I have done. Please help Jaime and Hallie to forgive me and to see that it was all a misunderstanding," Madison said through her whimpers.

All of a sudden Taylor came to her mind and she realized how angry she was with her, but she remembered what Miss Linda, their Sunday School teacher, told them about forgiveness. She knew she had to find a way to get past this hurt toward Taylor.

"And, Lord, please help me to forgive Taylor as well."

For the first time since yesterday, Madison felt a bit of peace.

Suddenly there was a knock at the door.

"Honey, can your mother and I talk to you for a minute?" her father asked.

"Yeah, come in," she answered in a quiet voice.

"Are you okay? You seemed a little upset a few moments ago," her mother said, looking concerned.

"I'm fine," Madison answered, squeezing her pillow.

"Well, you don't look fine," her father said. "You can tell us if something is going on. Maybe we can help you."

Madison's heart began to beat fast. She knew she had to say something, especially if she didn't go to Jaime's tonight for the sleepover.

"Well, yesterday after school, Taylor Nelson came out to us," Madison said quietly. "She told Hallie and Jaime that she found my journal on the floor. Then Taylor proceeded to blurt out what I wrote in it." She played with the tag on her purple pillow.

"Would you like to tell us what you wrote?" her mother asked, stroking Madison's hair.

"Not really," Madison answered, sniffling again. "I was angry that day, but Taylor failed to read all of it."

"All of it?" her father questioned. "There's more than what Taylor told them?"

"Yeah," Madison answered, handing her opened journal to her parents.

They read what Madison had written, then looked at her as if they were waiting for more of an explanation.

"Did you apologize to Jaime and Hallie?" her father asked, handing her a Kleenex. She took the tissue and dried her eyes.

"I tried, but they won't even speak to me," Madison said, wiping her nose. "They stormed off and wouldn't give me a chance to explain."

"What happened with Taylor?" her mother asked.

"Who cares?" Madison mumbled. "She's the one who started this whole thing."

"Listen, young lady! You know better than to blame someone else for what you did," her mother scolded. "Maybe Taylor shouldn't have told them what was in your personal journal, but you know better than to treat people with disrespect."

"I know. I'm really sorry, Mom and Dad," Madison said, looking down at the floor.

"Sweetheart, words can really hurt people. You have to be aware of what you say and how you say things," her mother replied. "Even if you write it and think they will never see it."

"I know," Madison said, looking at her mother.

"But," her father said, "I do believe that Hallie and Jaime will forgive you. They will come around. They are just hurting right now. And when they do, then you can show them what was actually written."

"But you don't understand," Madison said, looking at her parents. "I am officially uninvited to the sleepover tonight and the trip to the zoo tomorrow."

"Well, God has a way of working things out," her mother said, winking at her.

"He sure does," her father beamed. "Now you better get going, or you'll be late for school."

"Thanks for listening," Madison said, hugging both of her parents.

On her way downstairs, Madison grabbed her journal. She decided that Hallie and Jaime had to know the rest of the story. She only hoped they would hear what she had to say.

"Now let's go downstairs and finish breakfast," her mother said. "If we don't, your brothers may eat it all!"

Madison let out a deep sigh as she followed her parents downstairs. She was still upset, but she knew that today was going to be a better day because God would be with her.

As Madison walked to school, she began to pray about seeing her two friends.

"God, please let Hallie and Jaime forgive me. Lord, I know I messed up, but please help me to be able apologize to them. And, Lord, please help me to forgive Taylor for what she said as well. I know that she deserves forgiveness. I'm sorry for being upset with her. And thank you, Lord, for always listening to my prayers and answering me, regardless of the outcome. Amen."

Madison breathed a sigh of relief as she heard the birds chirping in the trees above her.

Even her brothers weren't bothering her right now. She was excited as she thought about the sleepover and trip to the zoo with Jaime and her family. Her smile, however, was replaced by a frown as she remembered that her best friends were mad at her. Yet Madison was determined that it was going to be a good day as she pushed the bad thoughts out of her head.

She had a brand-new day ahead of her. Suddenly, Madison couldn't wait to get to school to talk to Hallie and Jaime. She only prayed that her two best friends would talk to her.

When Madison arrived at school, she saw the girls standing near the playground. Ryan and Jason took off to meet their friends, and for an instant, Madison was jealous of them because their friends were happy to see them. Hallie and Jaime were whispering to one another when Madison walked up, and that made her very nervous.

"I can do this," she mumbled to herself. "God is with me."

"Oh, look, Hallie," Jaime said. "It's our so-called friend, Madison."

"Gee, I wonder what she wants, Jaime. Do you think it could be to insult us in person?" Hallie asked in a sarcastic voice.

Madison felt her face turn red. She was starting to lose confidence in apologizing. Just then the bell rang. Hallie and Jaime walked off without her, meeting up with Taylor. The three new friends strolled arm and arm, laughing as they went inside the school.

A pang of hurt struck Madison as she watched her friends replace her with Taylor. Madison was starting to get angry again, then remembered that it was in God's hands. In fact, Madison decided to wait until recess to talk to them. Maybe by then, she would feel a little more positive about things.

Madison drew in a deep breath as she entered the fourth grade classroom. A mixture of old crayons and new carpet wafted through the air. Madison felt sick as she walked forward to lay her crumpled homework in the basket on Miss Allsom's desk. She was a bundle of nerves as she walked to her desk.

Once again she glanced over at Hallie and Jaime and smiled. They glared back at her, which made her feel all alone again. She silently walked to the back of the classroom and hung up her coat and backpack in the coat closet.

The bell rang as she took her seat.

"This is harder than I thought, Lord. Please give me the courage to apologize," Madison silently prayed.

During the morning, Madison would sneak peeks toward her friends. They wouldn't even look toward Madison. However, a few times Taylor would smirk at her in a way that made Madison squirm.

At lunch she grabbed her tray of roast turkey, mashed potatoes with gravy, and peaches, and headed over to the lunch table she usually shared with her two best friends. Her heart was beating loudly, but she tried to ignore it. Her hands were shaking as she stood at the head of the table.

"Can I sit here?" Madison asked in a squeaky voice.

"Fine," Hallie said, rolling her fork through her lumpy mashed potatoes.

Madison set her tray down. She looked back and forth at Hallie and Jaime, who kept sharing glances without saying a word.

Madison couldn't take it anymore. "Look, guys, I'm sorry for what I wrote in my journal. I did say those things, but you didn't see what else I wrote," Madison said, looking at the turkey and gravy in front of her. "Here." Madison handed Hallie and Jaime the journal from underneath her hot tray. "I never meant to hurt you two. The day I wrote those hurtful things, I was upset. But late last night I read the rest of it. Taylor failed to read the whole thing to you," Madison finished.

"How do we know you didn't write this last night?" Hallie asked.

"Because you know I wouldn't do that," Madison answered.

"Fine, we'll read it," Jaime said, taking the journal.

She tried to read Hallie and Jaime's faces as they huddled together to read the entry. They looked at her, their faces softening.

"I felt left out because you both were signing up for soccer and neither one of you asked me to go with you," Madison added as she took a bite of her peaches.

"You don't even like soccer," Taylor smirked as she sat down across from Madison.

Madison ignored Taylor as she waited for her friends to answer her.

Hallie and Jaime looked at each other, then at Madison. Hallie smiled slightly.

"Madison, why didn't you just tell us how you felt?" Jaime asked.

"Yeah," Hallie chimed in. "We would have understood. And besides, you still could have shown up at the soccer field to cheer us on."

"I know," Madison sighed. "Hallie, Jaime, I really messed up. I understand if you never want to be friends again."

"Of course, we're still friends," Hallie said, running around the lunch table to hug Madison. "In fact, you better be at the sleepover tonight. It wouldn't be the same without you!"

"Yeah," Jaime said. "What would we do without each other?"

"Exactly," Hallie said. "Madison, you did hurt our feelings, but now that we saw for ourselves what was written, we believe that you were just upset."

"We have been friends for a very long time. And Hallie and I would miss you if you weren't our friend anymore," Jaime said, smiling.

"Really?" Madison exclaimed. "You really forgive me?"

"Of course, we do," Jaime said.

"Are you two seriously going to forgive her, for what she did?" Taylor asked.

"Yes!" Hallie and Jaime said together.

"But as for you, Taylor, what were you thinking scheming like that?" Jaime asked. "Were you trying to break our friendship up?"

"No, but I always believe in telling the truth. And the truth is, she wrote how she really felt about you. I thought it was only fair to share it with you," Taylor answered, flipping her hair off her shoulder.

"Well, you failed to read the rest of it," Hallie said, looking annoyed. "Why didn't you finish reading the rest of it?"

Taylor rolled her eyes. "Why should I? Can't you two see that Madison is nothing but a goody-goody?"

Hallie and Jaime leaned over the table and stared at Taylor.

The look must have frightened Taylor, because she suddenly blurted, "Oh, puleaze! I'm out of here."

"Taylor, wait," Madison spoke up. "Why do you hate me so much?"

"I don't hate you," Taylor said, looking sad. "It's just that you're so outgoing and nice to everyone, except me. I don't make friends very well, and then I noticed that you purposely try to leave me out of everything. After a while I thought I would get back at you for what you were doing to me."

"I'm sorry, Taylor." Madison said. "Sometimes I'm a little insecure. I never meant to hurt you." "In fact, apart from what happened with my journal, I really do want to be friends with you. I just never thought you liked me."

"You do want to be friends?" Taylor asked, slightly smiling.

"Of course. How can I stay mad at someone, when God has reminded me of all the times He's forgiven me when I've messed up?" Madison asked.

"Well, in that case, I think we should try to be friends," Taylor said, glancing up at Madison.

"Me too," Madison answered. "I would really like that."

Taylor replied, "And I wouldn't mind hearing more about God and His forgiveness."

"We'll tell you all about God when you come to my house for the sleepover," Jaime said. "As long as Hallie and Madison don't mind if you come along."

"Really?" Taylor's eyes widened. "I'm invited?"

"Of course, you are," Madison said, smiling at Taylor. "We are all friends now!"

The girls finished their lunch and headed out to recess. They began talking about their plans for the sleepover.

After school the girls headed to their homes to get packed for the sleepover at Jaime's.

Madison rushed around to gather what she needed for the weekend. She grabbed all her stuff and shoved it into the blue duffle bag. Her parents were happy to see that everything had worked out for Madison and her friends.

Later that evening Madison's father dropped her off at Jaime's. When she walked into Jaime's room, Taylor and Hallie were already there. And they were excited to see each other.

The girls ate junk food, played games, did each other's hair, and told Taylor all about God's love for her. As they got ready for bed, Taylor asked if she could pray and ask Jesus into her heart. The girls squealed in excitement. The three friends had Taylor repeat the prayer they had learned when each of them gave their lives to Jesus Christ.

Later on, as the four friends settled down to go to sleep, Madison couldn't help but smile. She not only learned that being a friend, keeps a friend, but she also learned that God answers prayers. As Madison closed her eyes, she looked up and quietly whispered, "Thank you, God! I love you!"

About the Author

Christy Mollet is a children's book author as well as a Copy Editor at *The Journal-News* in Hillsboro, Illinois. She loves to use her experiences to write stories in hopes of drawing readers closer to God. Her characters are each unique, but they come together in friendship to show God's love to those around them. Christy is a two-time kidney transplant recipient who is thankful for God's grace and mercy and her family.

CPSIA information can be obtained
at www.ICGtesting.com
Printed in the USA
LVHW012115211220
674733LV00004B/45